THE ROCKING HORSE

THE ROCKING HORSE
Juliet Harmer

COLLINS
PICTURE LIONS

First published in Great Britain 1986 by William Collins Sons & Co Ltd
First published in Picture Lions 1987
8 Grafton Street, London W1X 3LA
Picture Lions is an imprint of Fontana Paperbacks,
part of the Collins Publishing Group
Copyright © Text and illustrations Juliet Harmer 1986
Printed by Warners of Bourne and London

For
Jessie

Once upon a time, there was a beautiful rocking horse. He had a red and white saddle and bridle, a lovely furry mane and tail, and real little silver stirrups to put your feet in.

The little girl to whom he was given, played and played with him. Once, by mistake, she left him out in the garden all night. The little rocking horse was very frightened. But after a while, the moon came out and shone her silver beams on him and rocked him gently to sleep.

"I'm so sorry, Rocking Horse," said the little girl in the morning. "I will give you a good bath to make up."

She filled the bath up to the top. She tipped in a bottle of turquoise bubble bath and then she took off his saddle and bridle and lifted him as carefully as she could into the water.

He was beginning to look more cheerful already.

After his bath, the little horse was most carefully brushed and decorated. Now he felt much better.

That night he dreamt he was galloping along a beautiful beach with his little girl on his back.

One day, the little girl had to go away and the rocking horse was left in a dusty corner. He waited patiently for her to come back, but she didn't. Instead he heard strange voices.

"What about this old horse?"

"Oh, I don't think she'll want *that*."

And suddenly he was picked up, carried outside and left beside the dustbins with all the rubbish. A little tear rolled down the rocking horse's cheek.

The dustmen came. They cleared absolutely
everything away – including the little horse.
But he looked so sad that one dustman took pity
on him. "Perhaps you've been lost," he said.
"We'll leave you here."

And he put the little horse carefully in the
bushes at the side of the path.

The little horse waited. The snow came. He wondered what his wet white blanket was. He wished his little girl would come and find him.

Weeks and weeks went by. The snow melted and the sun appeared over the hill and felt warm on the little rocking horse's back. All around him, there were strange sounds. The birds were singing, and everywhere, bright flowers began to open. He felt something exciting was about to happen but he wasn't sure what it could be.

Then, one day, the little girl came running down the path. Suddenly she stopped. A peculiar hump was sticking up out of the grass.

"Oh dear," thought the little girl. For there, all tangled in the weeds and brambles, was the unmistakable shape of the little rocking horse.

The little girl set to work to make her rocking horse beautiful again.
"I'm afraid I shall have to do a small operation on you" she said. "It won't hurt much but it will mean a new head."
The little horse looked rather alarmed.
"Don't worry," said the little girl, "when I have finished, you are going to be the most beautiful rocking horse in the whole world."

By the time the little girl had to go to bed, the rocking horse was wearing one black jersey, one pair of black knickers, two pairs of black tights, one black wig, six black stockings, and a peacock feather to complete his magnificent appearance.

The little girl went to bed. In the night her father carried the rocking horse upstairs and put him by her bed. He fixed his best tie into a perfect bridle and onto the bridle he pinned a red rosette with 'First Prize' written on it in gold.

When she woke the next morning, the little girl was so happy to be home again and when she saw her horse, she was even happier. "Now you really *are* the most beautiful rocking horse in the whole wide world," she said. And she put her arms around his soft neck and smiled.

the end